Mouse's Christmas Gift

By Mindy Baker   Illustrated by Dow Phumiruk

ZONDERkidz

ZONDERKIDZ

Mouse's Christmas Gift
Copyright © 2018 by Melinda Baker
Illustrations © 2018 by Tiemdow Phumiruk

This title is also available as a Zondervan ebook.

Requests for information should be addressed to:

Zonderkidz, 3900 Sparks Drive SE, Grand Rapids, Michigan 49546

ISBN 978-0-310-75900-3

Art direction and design: Kris Nelson

Printed in China

18 19 20 21 22 /DSC/ 21 20 19 18 17 16 15 14 13 12 11 10 9 8 7 6 5 4 3 2 1

To Doug, Chelsea, Courtney, and Josiah.

–M.B.

For Stephanie and Dao.

–D.P.

Mouse shivered in the drafty sanctuary of the church. The room looked bleak and bare. *Where was Parson?* Mouse scurried over to Parson's empty study and glanced at the calendar. December 23. *Something wasn't right.*

As he crept back to the sanctuary, Mouse glanced around the room, and realized what was missing. In the storage closet, he burrowed through boxes, searching until he found the right one. *Could he arrange the delicate figurines?*

Pulling and prodding, lugging and lifting, Mouse worked until he finished the job. When he was done, sweet baby Jesus slept in the manger. Beside him stood Joseph and Mary, God's faithful servants. There was the magnificent angel that announced the greatest message of joy the earth would ever know. The lowly shepherds and sheep, chosen to hear and spread the good news, were there. And last, but not least, the wise men from the East, who followed the star and brought gifts to the King of kings.

But something still did not feel right. *Where could Parson be?* Mouse ducked through the crack in the wall. He raced through his tunnels until his wet nose poked into the small living quarters in the back of the church.

"Parson, your fever is worse," said his wife as she brushed her hand across his forehead.

Parson began to cough. "I guess I have no choice," he mumbled as he pulled the quilt over his thin, shivering frame.

Mouse watched Parson's wife nail a note to the door of the old church.
CHRISTMAS EVE SERVICE CANCELLED

Mouse's tail drooped. Parson had never cancelled a Christmas Eve service before! *Mouse had to do something! But what?*

Back to the boxes, he tripped and fell on something hard and made of wax. He had an idea! Mouse set a sturdy candle in the window of the old church and lit its wick. The glow filled the room. *But would anyone see it?*

That night, Mouse stared at the nativity in the soft
glow of the candlelight as he drifted off to sleep.

Across town, Alexander Stevens peered out his window into the starry night. The streets of the village looked deserted. The decorations stayed tucked away. Grim, worried villagers repeated the phrase, "No money for Christmas." Alexander sighed. *Did it really take money to celebrate Christmas?*

In the distance, he saw the silhouette of the old church, its strong steeple pointing to heaven. He blinked, then blinked again. *Was that a light in the window?*

While his parents slept, Alexander stepped softly out into the crisp air
and gathered pine branches and holly, forming a circle.

He ran to the church door and hung his meager wreath in place.
"Joy to the world," Alexander whispered to himself as he headed back home.

The next day, Lizzie Jenkins noticed Alexander's wreath on the door of the church.
She pointed and said to her sister, "That pine tree looks bare standing next to the wreath.
Let's tie our hair ribbons on its branches to decorate for Christmas."

From his forge, the blacksmith watched hair ribbons, quilting squares, and scraps of fabric appear on the tree as many passersby stopped to add a decoration. He began to heat and shape a piece of scrap metal into a shining star.

When the blacksmith thought no one was looking, he carried
a ladder over and set the star in its place.

Out her window, Widow Bartholomew's eyes studied the blacksmith as he placed the star on top of the tree. A smile crept onto her face. She looked in her cupboard and spotted the jar of strawberry jam she had saved for a special occasion. Then she set to baking bread.

That night, on Christmas
Eve, a small group of
villagers gathered in front
of the darkened church.
Mouse peered out the
window and his heart began
to pound. *They came!* He
raced up the doorframe and
unlocked the latch.

The townspeople talked
and whispered in front of
the church.

"It's been awhile since
I've been to church."

"Where's Parson and his
wife?"

"I think he's been ill."

They tried the door and
found it unlocked.

"I could light a fire in the stove," said the blacksmith.

"I've brought my bread and strawberry jam to share," added Widow Bartholomew.

The villagers sat in the pews and looked at each other. What next?

"We have our voices," said Mrs. Stevens.

So they began to sing:

"*O Holy Night, the stars are brightly shining,*

It is the night of our dear Savior's birth.

Long lay the world, in sin and error pining

'Till he appeared and the soul felt its worth.

A thrill of hope the weary world rejoices ..."

Parson heard the music
from his bed. *What was
going on?* He wrapped
himself in his quilt and
walked to the door, his wife
following behind.

As they entered the
chapel, someone began
reading from the Bible—
Luke chapter two: "In
those days Caesar Augustus
issued a decree that a
census should be taken of
the entire Roman world."
Parson sat down in a pew
and stared. *Why had the
people come? Who set up
the nativity? Had he left the
church unlocked?* He closed
his eyes and listened.

"I bring you good news that will cause great joy for all the people. Today in the town of David a Savior has been born to you; he is the Messiah, the Lord. This will be a sign to you: You will find a baby wrapped in cloths and lying in a manger."

Parson smiled. *Good news of great joy. The baby Jesus is the Savior for all people. He fills our greatest need.*

Mouse watched from his home in the wall, a smile on his face.
He nibbled a bit of bread and strawberry jam.
Christmas Eve. All was well.